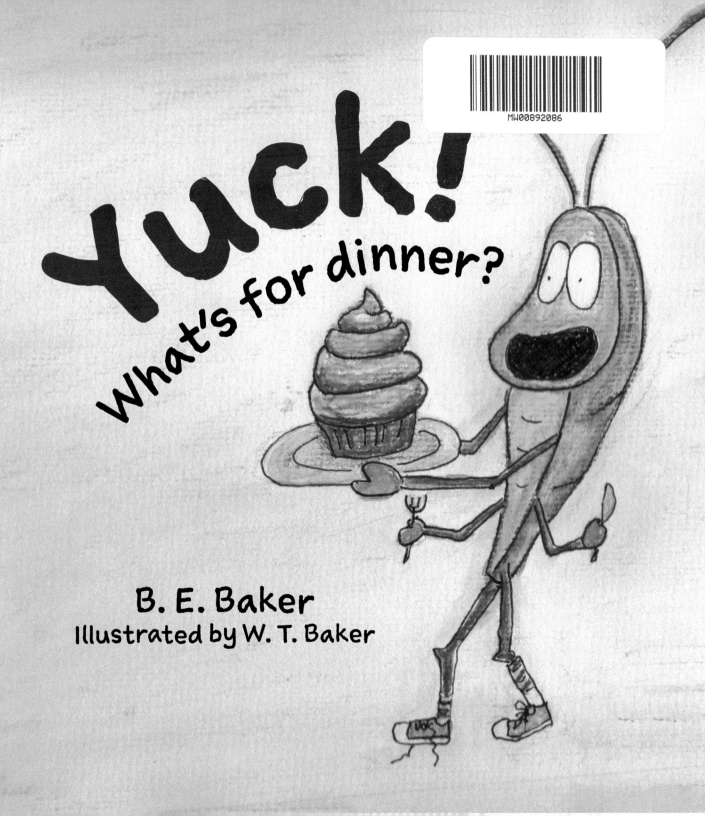

Yuck!
What's for dinner?

B. E. Baker
Illustrated by W. T. Baker

For Sammy.
We love you
now and forever,
exactly as you are.

Yuck! What's for dinner?

One fine spring
morning, a little
beetle popped out
of his safe place and
stepped into the
sunlight.

He blinked his eyes
and took a good
look around.

"You're awake! You're finally awake!" A much larger beetle clapped her hands and jumped in the air.

"**W**ho are you?" he asked.

She pulled the small beetle close and squeezed him. "Your name is Max," she said, "and I am your mother. I've been counting the days until I could meet you."

4

" I'm happy to meet you too," Max said. "But I have a funny feeling here in my middle. Do you know why?"

"Oh, that means you're hungry," his mother said. "That's good news. The more you eat, the more you grow."

5

Grow? Max liked the idea of growing...
"What do we like to eat?" Max asked.
"Well, we're dung beetles sweetheart,
so we eat—"

6

"Oh, I know! Do we eat nice, juicy peaches?"

"Uh, no. Like I said, we are DUNG beetles. So we eat—"

7

Max leapt into the air. "I know—
popcorn. No, spaghetti!"

Max's mother frowned. "It's very rude
to interrupt. You're only a baby, so I'll
forgive you, but no. We don't eat those
things. We eat dung."

"We're named after what we eat?" Max scratched his head. "And what in the world is DUNG?" His eyes lit up. "Is it a kind of ice cream?"

"It most certainly is not ice cream," his mother said. "Dung is. . ."

"...poop."

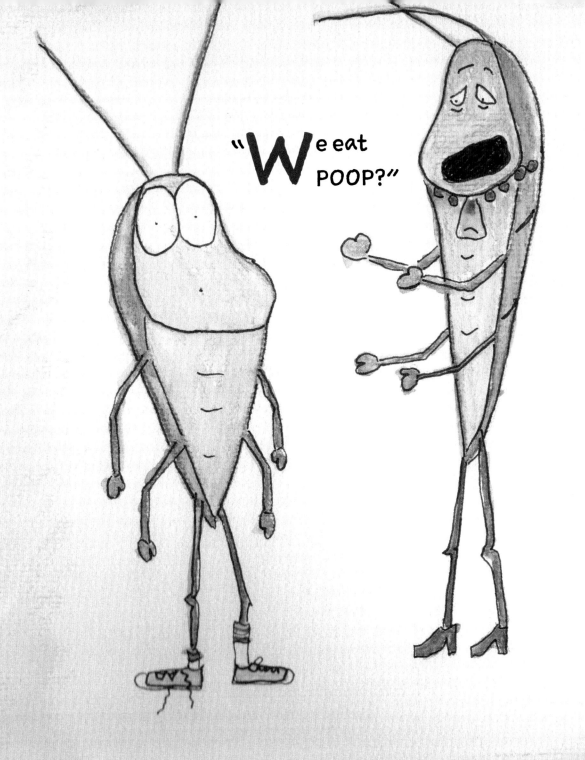

"**D**on't look so alarmed," said Max's mother. "Lots of critters eat strange things. Pigs eat garbage. Birds eat worms. Frogs eat flies. Hedgehogs eat snails, and vultures eat dead stuff."

"**A**nd furthermore, you're very lucky," his mother said. "Because we live in dung beetle paradise. Look around!"

15

"Oh I'm grateful, really. But I don't think I can eat that."

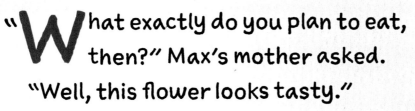

"What exactly do you plan to eat, then?" Max's mother asked. "Well, this flower looks tasty."

Before his mother could object, Max took a bite, chewed, and swallowed. "Why are you looking at me like that?" he asked.

"I'm hoping that flower doesn't kill you," his mother said.

But Max was fine.

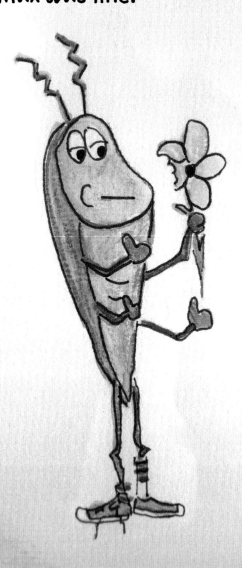

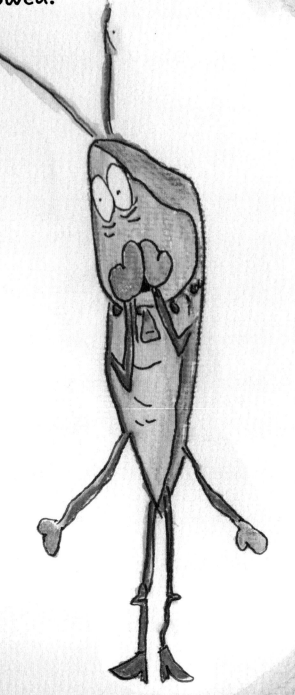

The next day his mother rolled a greenish poop ball across the yard to where he was sitting. "Your grandmother's favorite food was always chicken poop," she said. "Why don't you try it?"

"Uh, thanks, but I just grabbed my dinner." Max held up his dandelion flower. "It's so fluffy. I'm sure it will taste great."

"You are a dung beetle, Max. You will have to eat dung eventually."

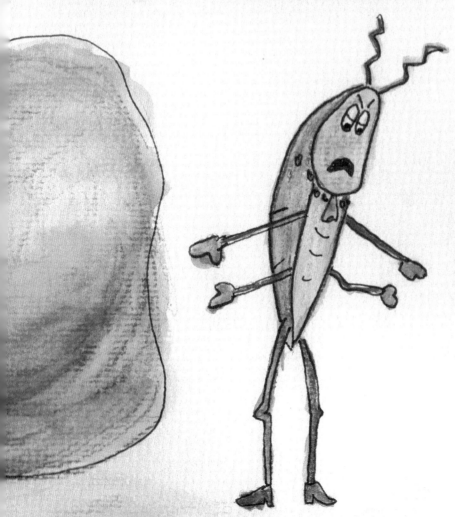
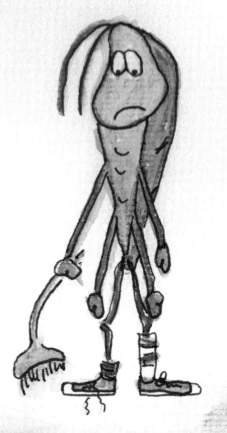

His mother pointed. "Try a bite.
You might like it."
  Max didn't want to be rude, but
he *really* didn't want to eat any.
"No thank you."

Max's mother grabbed two leaves and a skinny mushroom and pushed them together. "Maybe a sandwich, then."

Max squinted. "Is there poop in that sandwich?"

"Of course there is," Max's mother said.

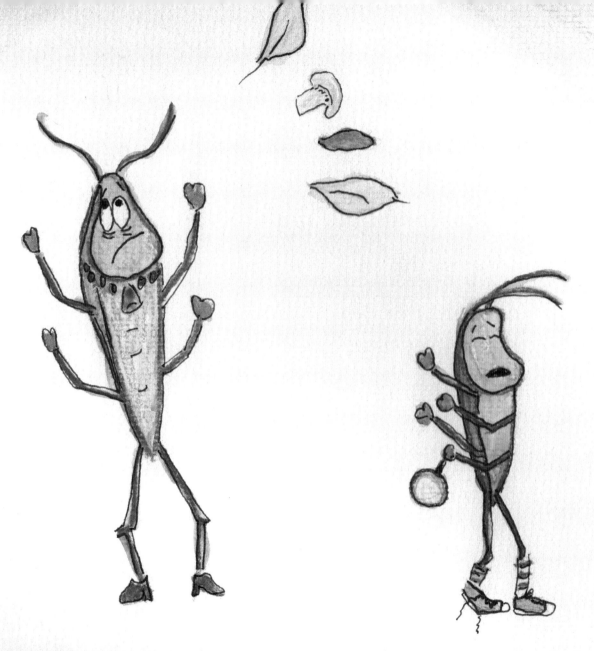

"Then thank you," Max said, "but I'm not interested."
Max's mother threw her hands in the air.

The next day, Max's mother had waited long enough. She grabbed Max's arms and marched him into the back pasture. She pointed at a mountain of poop balls. "This is horse poop. Manure is fresh, it comes pre-rolled into balls, and it's vegetarian. It's ridiculously good, and you will TASTE it."

Max tried to squirm away, but his mother stomped her foot and scowled.

Max grabbed a handful of warm, stinky manure... and...
he popped it into his mouth.

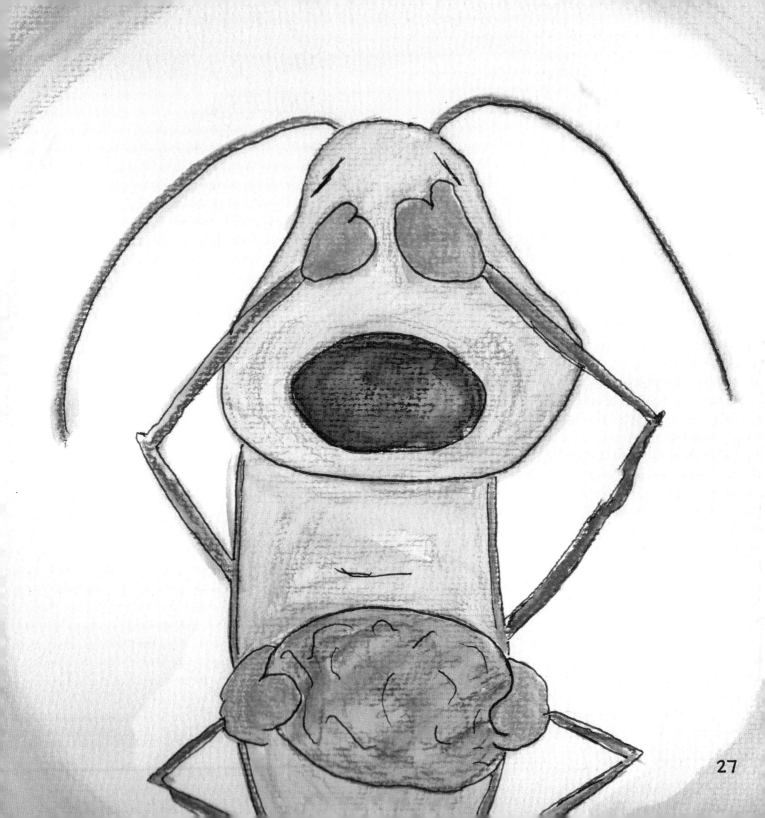

Max's tummy
didn't like it.
Not at all.

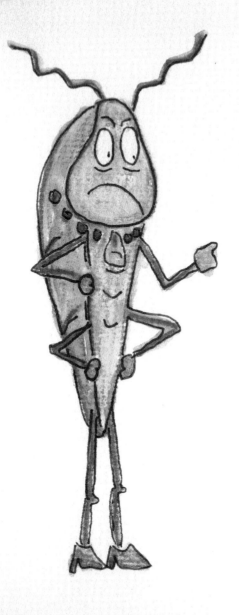

His mother was not pleased.

29

B ut she didn't give up. "We just haven't found the right kind yet."

Max followed his mother a long way to a brightly lit store.

"This is your dad's favorite place to eat." She pointed at the shop window. "It's not great to eat here every day, but as an occasional treat, it's fine."

Max tried one bite of each thing on the menu, but he didn't like any of it.

His mother still didn't give up. Max dutifully tried all the things his mother shoved at him: cat, chicken, cow, and dog poop.

They all tasted like they smelled.

Not good.

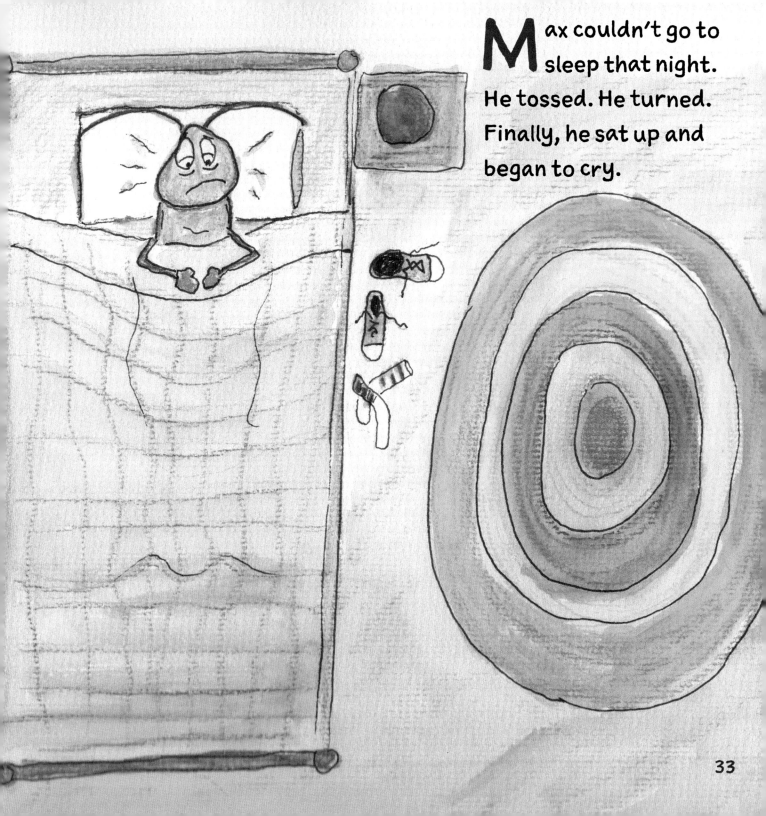

Max couldn't go to sleep that night. He tossed. He turned. Finally, he sat up and began to cry.

His mother heard a strange noise and came to see what it was. When she saw Max's tears, she sat on the edge of his bed.

"I want to be a good dung beetle. I want to be like you," Max said.

His mother hugged him. "We will figure this out. You are a good dung beetle. I want you to be a healthy one, too."

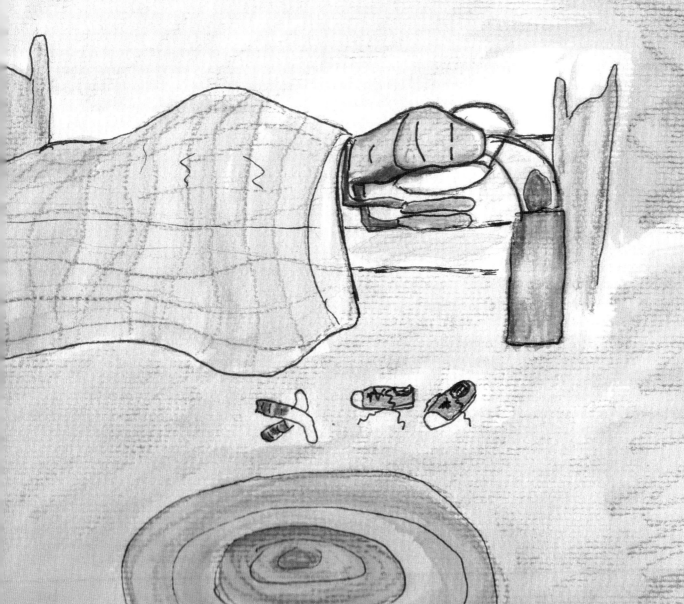

Max finally went
to sleep.

35

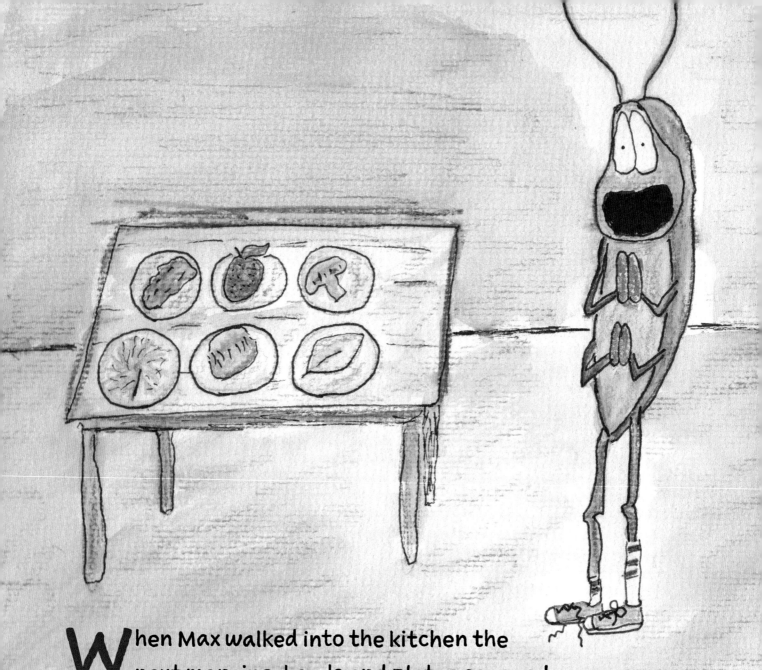

W hen Max walked into the kitchen the
next morning, bowls and plates covered
the counter. Max couldn't believe his eyes, because
not a single one held any poop.

" I 've done some research," said his mother. "In fact, I stayed up all night, and I discovered that you can eat several things that are NOT poop and still be healthy."

Max's lip trembled. "But I want to be like you."

"We don't have to eat the same things to be family," his
mother said. "And I love you just the way you are."

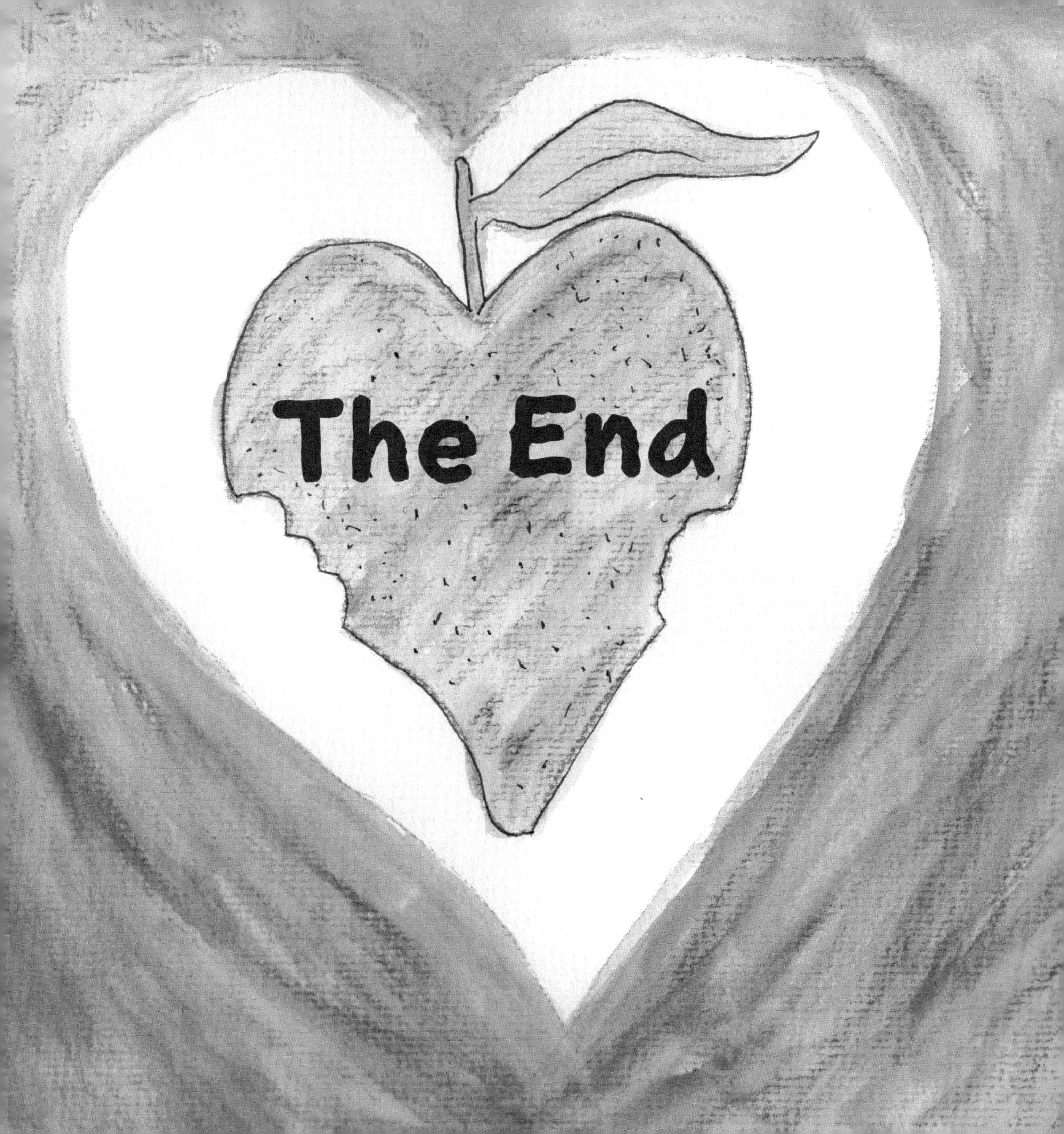
The End

Made in the USA
Las Vegas, NV
04 November 2020